T0166048

Flies without Wings

Ardien Blu

iUniverse, Inc.
New York   Bloomington

iUniverse books may be ordered through booksellers or by contacting:

iUniverse
1663 Liberty Drive
Bloomington, IN 47403
www.iuniverse.com
1-800-Authors (1-800-288-4677)

ISBN: 978-1-4401-5595-6 (sc)
ISBN: 978-1-4401-6561-0 (ebook)

Printed in the United States of America

iUniverse rev. date: 07/16/2009

I dedicated this project to my husband and son
who are my reason for being and my inspiration to fly.
Thank you mom for the direct and indirect teachings .

Thank you GOD for the introduction.

"Circumstance and Consequence"

"Naïve, go in there and wake yo daddy up so he can eat,*"* momma yelled from the kitchen. She was preparing dinner while he lay across her bed DRUNK again. This was a familiar scene in our household. When he wasn't drinking he was a perfect father; attentive, funny and nice sometimes. We didn't get many opportunities to have this view of him though. Alcohol was always his solace and when he got drunk things could get bad; real bad.

Momma named me Naïve because she once said it reflected how she felt after getting pregnant with me at the early age of seventeen. Although she thought too that it was pretty and different, it would prove to be a name I'd grow to hate. It would never, in my mind, be a representation of me or who I would be in life.

I had learned earlier in childhood, by age nine that John was not my real father but he was all that I knew. That was my "diddy" as momma used to tease me in saying and I was his little girl. The story is that my biological father, as I would learn later in life, was a different kind of man; different being the operative word. I never knew him so John would have to do as a substitute for now.

For almost two years after momma married John, it was just the three of us: me, Momma and John until my brother came along. Momma named him John Jr. By the time I was five or six my mother and John's relationship would change and take us from place to place and situation to situation routinely without fail. There seem to be fights between them all the time. It seemed as if alcohol and unemployment would increasingly invite themselves to our house and make themselves comfortable. John Jr. and I would soon grow to accept this as "the norm" and just live with it. John's excessive drinking often lead to him loosing jobs and his side hustles would prove to be temporary leaving us once again to be what I would call "on the run."

As a child, we never stayed in on place too long. I never knew why we moved so much at first but by the time I was nine, we'd seen most of the South briefly. We saw more of the highway than most kids I knew. It became a game for John Jr. and me. We saw it as an adventure every time we'd hit the road, off to a new place. I remember the long rides in the car where John Jr. and I would make up games to past the time away in the back seat of the car. Our favorite was "That's My Car." We would each choose a color and claim any car that passed by with our chosen color for points. Being the oldest I always claimed "winner."

Those rides would prove to be the catalyst for my belief that a person has to mobilize themselves to get somewhere in life. Otherwise, grass grows under your feet. Those adventures where some of the happiest times of my life. In that back seat you could watch the road out of the window and dream. The best thing about it being just me and John Jr. meant no one had to fight for a window seat. Out of that window we'd look up to the sky and pick clouds that looked like something familiar. One time, I thought I saw God himself.

New places brought about new friends. Some were nice and some not so nice. It was in Tennessee where I discovered that I hated boys at the tender age of seven. In the south, all of the school aged kids rode the long yellow bus to school. The schools were always at such a distance from where you lived that it had to be this way. Having your own car was a luxury most couldn't afford. The bus driver would pick you up in front of your house or a designated spot each day. If you weren't ready when the bus got there you were good as absent because you'd have no other choice but to stay at home that day. There was no second bus coming and the bus driver wasn't coming back for you either. Momma made sure we were on time everyday. She did not believe in missing the bus or school. Death was your only excuse she'd say.

She also believed that little girls should always look appropriate-in dresses. The hair ribbons and socks must match. I was a tom boy and hated dresses of any kind but she made me wear them anyway. One day, Junior Cobb, a boy who lived down the road with his grandma decided to challenge me. He liked me and every morning at the bus stop he would speak. Like I said, I didn't like boys much and today would be the day he'd find out why. "Hey Navi … " he'd say with that silly smirk on his face. He couldn't pronounce my name right so he came up with this silly nickname I suppose. Hell, truth be told, nobody could say my name right. I would learn later that this would become an issue for most. "**Hey Junior**," I'd say with an attitude. I always rolled my eyes afterwards for the full affect. It didn't matter though. He would just smile or sometimes just laugh out loud as if something were funny.

It was picture day and momma had bought me a new dress to wear to school. As expected, the sox and hair ribbons to match. I must admit, if I were into dresses, it would be cute to me too. The minute I lifted my leg to board the bus, Junior lifted the back of my dress! The other kids standing in line to board the bus starting laughing. My brother began laughing too. After pulling my foot back from his chest and soon after John Jr. helped him up off the ground, Junior had the nerve to say, "I just wanted to see if yo drawers matched too." The kids laughed again and I quickly walked past the driver and took a seat at the back of the bus; the window seat. I declared that day that I hated boys forever and I knew it wouldn't be the last time I'd be humiliated by one.

We moved to Texas by the time I was eleven. The saying is that things grow big in Texas but no one warned of how hot it was. Texas would become a lasting memory for me for more than one reason even though, as usual, we wouldn't be here long.

We moved in with momma's uncle, Henry. He was a nice man. I had never met him before. His family seemed nice too. He had kids who where already grown so there wasn't much playing going on inside the house except for John Jr. and me. We stayed respectful though. Momma wouldn't have it any other way. She did not play when it came to discipline.

One time John Jr. got popped in the chops for speaking out of turn, when "grown folks are talking." I thought momma had loosened some teeth she'd hit him so hard. Like I said, momma did not play when it came to discipline. It wouldn't be the last time John Jr. would get smacked; he was hard headed. It was clear to me though; never speak until I was spoken to. That was one of momma's rules. Being the oldest wasn't so hard until John Jr. would get into trouble about something. That was most of the time and I'd usually get yelled at for not watching him. We were only a year and six months apart. He knew better but he seemed to enjoy pressing momma's buttons. If she told me once, she'd have to tell him twice and usually if she had to say it more than once, you're as good as dead! I believe I got as many whippings as John Jr. just by association.

Uncle Henry's daughter Kim lived at home with he and his wife. She was the youngest of his kids, just sixteen. She was pretty with long hair and a nice girly shape and she smoked things. She'd gotten herself pregnant a year earlier and had a child. She wasn't married to the father so I think that's why she was still at home. We got along well and I very quickly began to look to her as a big sister figure. It wouldn't be long before that would change forever and prove to be one more of my life's experiences.

John quickly fell in place as well. He and Uncle Henry's wife discovered they enjoyed the same poison. Soon his actions would expose our life to strangers once again. A stint of unemployed woes and dried up hustles would again take its toll. Getting drunk with company now became an everyday past time. One day Uncle Henry announced to John that he'd try to get him a job at his employer's grocery. He helped momma get a job too, cleaning white folk's houses. After three weeks, John lost the job and momma continued cleaning three days a week. Seventy five dollars a day is what she made. Good jobs were hard to find in Texas unless you worked at the Refinery but, you'd have to" know somebody" to get in.

For a while life seemed good. We enrolled in school and made new friends. This is what we did every time we landed somewhere. John Jr. and I were used to it and learned to just embrace it.

Kent Broussard was a boy in my class. I quickly learned that he lived just up the street from Uncle Henry's house. I liked him. He was cute. Plus, he had a strange name like mine. "My sister likes you," John Jr. blurted out during our usual walk home from school one day. I reacted by slapping the back of his head. As usual, everybody thought it was funny but me. I was embarrassed to no end. I didn't want Kent to know I liked him. I said nothing else the rest of the way home.

I was a skinny, leggy girl with braids all over my head. Medusa is what they'd call me in school. Momma thought it was a cute hair style. Truth be told, she only did it because it bought her time in between washes and combing. I had long nappy hair when it wasn't pressed and I didn't think it was cute at all. I didn't think I was cute and I certainly didn't think Kent thought I was either. My luck would quickly change though. That day, after homework, we started going together.

One day after returning home from school, momma announced that we would be moving into our own place. She had already begun packing the little stuff we had. I would later come to understand the abruption. Nobody would say but, based on an overheard conversation; it had something to do with John and Kim. We packed our things and moved that weekend.

The new apartment was small; a kitchen, living room and two bedrooms. John Jr. would have to sleep on the couch for what would turn out to be the next eight months. We'd share my closet space. The Alex Hailey Roots series would air for the next eight nights and everybody in the house would watch. Every day we'd hurry to finish homework so we'd be able to watch it with momma. She'd always explain the parts we'd have questions about. John watched with us the first night. He never watched again. Momma would say he was out working. Of course we knew when he'd return he'd be drunk and the arguments would begin like clock work. He never needed a reason to be pissed about anything when he was drinking. Everything seemed to aggravate him. He'd pick on us for the simplest of things. "God dammit, didn't I tell you to fix me a plate? Take your ass to bed!" he'd say. It seemed to always be my fault for everything. Momma would send me off to fix the plate and then I'd have to ask John's permission to stay up a while longer to see the end of Roots that night. Sometimes to keep him from getting angrier she'd just make us both go to bed. I guess that was her way of keep things even between John Jr. and me.

Eight months later I arrived home from school to find packed boxes all around the apartment. With an attitude, I slowly walked past momma and mumbled "we moving agin?" She responded, "you trying to be a smart ass huh?!" I continued to my room and closed the door behind me. I took a seat on my bed next to the window and stared out.

I looked down at the window sill at a few dead flies that had accumulated. Most were dead because of me and John Jr. Looking for something to do when we got bored, we'd catch them, pull off their wings and watch them buzz and flip flop all over the place. It was funny to watch. Today though, I can almost understand how they must've felt. On top of hearing the news that we were moving, at recess I heard that Kent liked Cortney.

"Second Chances"

We moved to another town about twenty miles from Uncle Henry. He'd visit from time to time but we'd hardly visit him. Momma continued cleaning houses to make ends meet. By now she'd added two more locations to her route. Every once in a while she'd take me with her to help out. The first time I went to work with her I was in such awe of how white folks were living. We came from Chicago where the houses were mostly apartments on our side of town; people living above you or below. All of the buildings were located next to one another. This was different. Most homes were walk-ins with attached garages and laundry rooms. Where we've lived, you park on the street and you wash your clothes a few blocks down at the laundry mat. Here, you had a laundry room a few steps from the kitchen or in a special part of the house. I was sure this was how I wanted to live. I was convinced that I would own one and not be the maid of one some day.

I hated that momma had to resort to this kind of work; this kind of survival. It was 1978. Slavery had been abolished a long time ago. She was a smart woman in my eyes and had greater potential. There were times back home when she held jobs that required suits, shoes and pantyhose. This was all John's fault I thought. This didn't look or feel right to me. It felt like we were back in the days of Roots or something. I would soon understand why she did it and why very soon she'd pack us up and move us back home.

Things seem to get tougher for us this time. This situation was much different than ever before. John was out of work but was making some money as a car mechanic off and on. All the money that he didn't drink up, he brought home to contribute to expenses. One by one our utilities were turned off from non payment and several times we dodged the landlord by not answering the door when he came knocking. Momma made about seventy-five dollars per house but that wasn't nearly enough to feed two kids and pay bills, but she tried. We never shopped down all the aisles of the grocery store because she always knew what she could afford to get. Once when our lights were turned out, momma bought a bag of ice to keep the milk for cereal cold in the ice cooler John used for the fishing trips with Uncle Henry. She would sometimes use the barbeque grill on the enclosed back porch to cook meals. For the exception of the smoke in the house, it worked out pretty good for a while. To avoid wearing wrinkled clothes to school, we'd place them between the mattress and box spring while we slept. Momma always seemed to make the best of our bad situations. When the electric got turned off homework would be done by candlelight until John got a bright idea to hook up a car battery to a headlight and when the gas was cut off, John found a way to start it up again too. It worked for a while until the gas company found out. He could be resourceful when he wanted to be when he was sober. When things got as bad as they could get, momma began avoiding Uncle Henry. She was embarrassed and wanted no one to know how really bad things had gotten.

John Jr. made friends quickly in the neighborhood. He was friendly like that. We never brought friends into the house so he'd usually have company on the porch. That was one of momma's rules.

I was sitting on the porch one day when a girl walked by. She said hi, I said hi. People are really polite in the south. They'll speak even when they don't know you. Her name was Dorothy and we would eventually become best friends. Blood sisters even and I would soon learn that she used to be the girlfriend of the boy next door, Carl

Dunbar. Carl was friends with my brother and I liked him. We soon became more than friends, after I cleared it with Dorothy. I didn't want to be his girlfriend if she still liked him. Even though it was long before I came along and they were much younger, I needed to make sure I wasn't trespassing. I grew to like Carl and his family and I tried very hard to appear normal despite the turmoil going on at my house. I hoped they hadn't figured out every time the utilities were off or even recognized the landlord coming by so much. I wondered if they ever heard the arguments thru open windows or noticed the smoke from the grill. If they did, they never said anything.

Every evening Dorothy would walk down the rode from her house to mine and we'd sit on the porch to talk. On this day she wanted to walk to the park instead because she wanted to talk to me about something important. I must admit I was nervous. Was she gonna tell me that she wanted Carl back? Or maybe that they where seeing each other all along? We walked past the gate and into the park. "Navie, I don't know how to say this," she started. I got a little nervous. Carl was only the second boy I'd ever liked. In fact, I thought I loved him. "We're blood sisters right? I mean, we can talk about anything, right?!" she asked. She was making me more nervous the more she spoke, swaying her foot back and forth in the grass as if she were looking for something dropped. She began to speak. "I saw your father coming from the store yesterday and he was trying to get me to get in the car with him. I told him I was okay, that I could walk. He called me over to the car and asked me if I wanted to take a ride with him. Girl, I got scared and ran off. I can't come back over yo house no mo." My mouth dropped. I couldn't believe what she was saying. "Was he drunk?" I asked knowing that I knew the answer. When wasn't he? "It looked like he was. He had a bottle in the car," she said.

I never said a word to momma about it. Dorothy would eventually stop coming by and John would never be looked at by me the same way again. John was messing up everything. He made me loose my best friend. Why couldn't my momma see that he was no good? If I said anything it would mean trouble. I was afraid of John and what he might do so I decided to keep it to myself. Momma would eventually grow tired of our mess of circumstances and would soon make an announcement to John Jr. and I that we would be moving back to Chicago. We would be sent first by train and she and John would follow thereafter.

Hating John increasingly became easy for me. Joy and happiness could hardly find a welcome when he was around. Momma never said it but, I got the feeling she felt the same too. She seemed to be the happiest when she was away from him and I truly believed deep down inside she really would be. I just couldn't understand what kept her from completely walking away from him for good. This could not be love. Was she crazy or as scared of him as I was? I would close my eyes sometime and just wish he would die. Simply go away for good. Forever!

It was 1979 and we were back in Chicago. We took up temporary residence with momma's sister and her kids. A few years earlier her husband, son and a cousin would be killed by a family member. The family hardly ever talked about it or what really happened and we just kind of knew not to ask. Momma said she wanted to come back to help her sister. I think she used the tragedy as an excuse to get John's buy in so we could come back home. We got enrolled in school right away. I would start my first year in high school. John Jr. started in elementary, eighth grade. He was excited too because in Chicago, you graduate out of eighth grade into high school. I missed that chance. In Texas, they just pass you on to the next grade. I was happy to just be back with my family. At home, things would be a lot better I hoped.

"Wolf in Sheep's Clothing"

Momma and John had arrived and momma's sister found a way to make us all fit comfortably in her home as best she could. It was tight but we all managed for a while. Momma and John shared space in the basement, I shared a room with her girls and John Jr. found a couch somewhere. To this day I bet he hates couches. Holidays would be fun here because my aunt loved them and she had a knack for making things fun and exciting. Everybody would come to her house. It was where the fun was. For once, it felt okay to be a kid and for once I could feel like a girl again.

I fell in love for the second time with a friend of my cousin. His name was Donald Jameson. He lived across the street from my aunt's house and we were in the same grade. I was almost fifteen and no one could tell me that it wasn't true love, although everyone tried. Donnie and I grew closer and as all of the pressures of having sex surrounded us, we decide to wait until I was ready. Little did I know that it didn't mean necessarily that Donnie would wait for me. I'd heard a rumor or two about him being with others but he'd always manage to convince me that it was a lie, I'd believe him and life would go on being wonderful again.

After a year or so, we would eventually move from my aunt's house and into our own place. It wasn't very far from her so, I could continue going to my school, John Jr. his. I wouldn't see Donnie as often as before but, we managed to make time for each other and he continued to wait for me.

That same year, a niece of momma's called and asked if she could stay with us for a while until she got back on her feet. She'd lost her job and was losing her place too. Momma thought it was a good idea sense she was now working nights and needed someone to stay with us in her absence. To keep an eye on things she said. John was out of a job again and was up to his usual. Momma thought the arrangement seemed to be the best for all so she said yes! My cousin moved in and life seemed to be fine for a while.

Momma put in a roll-away bed so we could share my room. It was cool to have a roommate, a big sister. John Jr. was okay to have around as my brother all these years but, truth-be-told I always wanted a sister. During our episodes of "playing house" when John Jr and I were younger, I'd always dress him up in my clothes. He was the cutest fat girl I'd ever seen with dress, socks and ribbons to match.

It had already been two months since she had arrived when things started changing. One night I awoke to hear her whispering anxiously. "John, you better git out of here." At first I thought I was dreaming or maybe she was being sneaky talking to someone on the phone. Momma didn't allow phone calls after a certain hour. She had told my cousin this once before. Said it ran up her phone bill. I didn't dare let her know I was awake. Without hesitation she said it again. "John, I'm not playing with you, leave me alone. Git out of here!" By this time I had figured out that she was not on the phone. She was talking to John who was now on his knees crawling to her beside. I panicked. I had to think of something so I coughed, loudly. The cough startled John and he slowly backed out of the room.

The next morning I said nothing. My cousin said nothing. I went to school. By the time I returned home, she had most of her stuff packed. She was leaving she said. She had made arrangements to stay with our grandmother until she could find somewhere else to go. I began crying as she continued to pack her things. She turned around towards me. "What you crying for?" she said. "What's wrong?" I didn't want to tell her what I saw and heard and I didn't want her to leave me either. "I saw my diddy in here last night. I heard what you said to him and I saw what he was trying to do. That's why I coughed so that he would leave you alone." She looked at me with surprise and made me promise not to say anything to anybody. She said it would cause too much trouble. By now I'd stopped crying. I looked at her and said "I'm not staying here. What if the next time he does it to me? I'm going with you." My cousin wasn't that much older than me and from her reaction it seemed to me that she had lived this nightmare before. I wasn't going to ask her though. All I knew was that I was not going to be next. It was Friday and momma had already left for work. There was no time to debate it or ask for permission to go and all I knew was that I wasn't staying behind. John Jr. knew nothing about what had happened but when he saw me leaving, he asked where I was going, I simply said I was going to our grandmother's with my cousin.

When momma got home John Jr. couldn't wait to tell. Momma called Granny's house mad as hell and made me come home. She tore me a new one when I got home. You don't do anything or go anywhere without her permission. That was her rule. I prayed a lot after that. Every night I suppose. I needed someone to protect me. Momma seemed to not know how because she wasn't doing a good job at it in my eyes. I was scared and convinced my time would come. And it did.

A few months had past. My birthday was coming up and soon I'd be sweet sixteen. Donnie and I were doing okay although we seemed to have more issues and less relationship. I had decided though, at sixteen I'd be ready. I wanted him to be my first. That was my plan.

One evening after finishing homework early, I decided to watch t.v. on the enclosed back porch. I put on my favorite flannel pajamas that momma had bought for me. A simple flannel floor length gown. It was warm and cozy. I'd often wear it when I knew I'd be watching television on the enclosed back porch because it could get pretty drafty. Momma was at work, John Jr. was doing homework in his room and John? Well, with momma working nights, he was subject to be anywhere doing anything except working.

The back door opened and I heard him stumble up the stairs to our second floor apartment. He came through the door drunk as ever and crashed on the couch almost crushing me. I moved over. "Hey diddy" I said, afraid to say any more. "Whatchudoin," he said in a drunken slur. "Just watching t.v.," I said as I got up to walk out of the room. He saw me and told me to wait, to sit back down. I did as I was told but after what had happened to my cousin, I tried never to be in the same room with John alone. Often times I tried not to talk to him either even when momma was around. I'm sure she sensed something wasn't right but, she never said a word.

"I got a question for you. You and Donnie having sex yet?" My heart started pounding as if it would come right out of my chest. Reminiscent of how I felt the night I saw him on his knees in my room with my cousin, I wasn't sure what to say or what to do. John Jr. had his radio up so loud he wouldn't hear anything if I yelled out. I turned toward the t.v., afraid to look at him and said, "Nooo ... and I don't think that's something you should be asking me." He laughed and said, "I'm just playing wit you." Then suddenly without warning, "You wanna try it with me?" I jumped up and excused myself and walked swiftly to my room. "I knew it ..." I kept saying in my mind. I knew my turn was coming. I was nervous, scared and confused. I had no idea what to do next. Before I could figure it all out, before I could close my door behind me, he stumbled his drunk ass to the threshold of my doorway. There he stood, pants unfastened with penis in hand. I screamed for him to get out of my room. I had hoped that John Jr heard me. I had hoped that he would make a noise, cough or something but, he never did .He never would hear me because as it turns out, he'd fallen asleep studying. What seemed like an hour happened in a few minutes. John threatened that if I told, he'd kill me and then he was gone. I jumped from my bed and locked my door and waited for momma to come home. I didn't sleep that night and for many nights after. My solace was the scissors I kept under my pillow and I never said a word about it to anyone. I questioned what I might have done to provoke this. Was it the gown? Maybe I wasn't dressed appropriately around him. Maybe being flannel, it wasn't thick enough. I wasn't shapely. Never was. My breasts were small. I had no butt. Why would he look at me in this way? I would come to understand later that none of this would be my fault and had nothing to do with how I looked. I couldn't tell my momma. John told me if I told he'd kill me. I believed him but, more importantly I believed he would hurt her too. The fights over the years became more intense. Perhaps it was because momma was beginning to fight back. Over the years she would be cut, he would be jailed and I was almost kidnapped by this fool. I knew what he was capable of and I needed to protect us all. So I never said a word to her about it.

The relationship between momma and John would eventually run its course and run out of steam. It was the finale. She'd decided it was time to leave for good. By now she had already met someone else and plans to start anew where already in the works. The new guy turned out to look just like John to me. With all that I had gone through, perhaps every man from now on would. Nevertheless, I didn't take to him at all at first.

My decision to give up my virginity to Donnie really wasn't a big deal after all. Afterwards I wondered what was the big deal anyway. I believed too much had happened in my life to understand the beauty of it all. We didn't last much longer after that because I had forever been changed and my opinion of men was at an all time low and LOVE was overrated. My attitude had changed towards momma too. We argued and disagreed as often as night turned to day. The new guy had moved in with us by now and things had already begun changing. He provided financially and soon he would ask her to quit her job for good. I wanted her to be happy. For as much as she had suffered, I wanted for her, an equal amount of happiness. I just wasn't sure if it was with him. For me, our family had not healed before a new chapter had already begun. I always believed that momma was never a bad person, just a person making some bad decisions. Yet, I never stopped to think of what she might have truly gone through emotionally with John. I could only think about what John had taken from me.

Some years had past by when I got the news from mom that John was found dead. I got the call at work one day. "Hey baby … I just called to tell you that they found yo daddy last night." Customarily, this would not be the most appropriate way to break this kind of news. "Is he dead?" I asked, rolling my eyes with unconcern. She confirmed with a yes and I assured her that I would not attend a funeral for him but that I would like to go to the funeral home to make sure that it was him. I wanted to make sure the bastard was dead! She agreed and made the arrangements to do so. That day, I realized that God was real and he heard my prayer. I knew it wasn't right but I'd prayed for so long that He would make John disappear. For good! John was evil and I hoped he'd fry in Hell.

The night momma finally left John, he had jumped her. Beat her like I'd never seen before. I'd later learn that the new guy was the reason for it. John had suspected an affair of some kind. He might have been right for all that I knew but once again John took revenge for it by setting our apartment on fire during the separation. He had called me to inform me of his plans. With hell in his heart and the devil on his tongue he said, "You better call ya momma 'cause I'm finnah burn this mothah fuckah down." I knew he was drunk and he meant it. I called momma to warn her but by the time she got there, the apartment was destroyed. It was said that he started the fire in my room, the hallway leading to their bedroom as well as he and momma's room. She had mustered the strength to leave his crazy ass but he didn't make it easy for any of us. He called with threats; showed up where he wasn't invited. Then one day the threats suddenly stopped. The phone calls stopped too and the next time we heard, John was dead.

"When you get home from school today, I'll be there to take you to our new house," momma called to say one morning before I had left for school. We'd been staying with one of momma's sisters after the fire: John Jr and I that is. Momma had taken residence elsewhere for the time being. My money was on the new guy though her story was told differently. "Where are we moving to now? I don't wanna change schools," I said, confused and upset. "Just be ready when I get there. Tell John Jr. too." She and I weren't getting along real well. This was the first time she'd ever left us to live in a different place than where she was. We'd always go where she went but this time was different. There was something about this new guy I just didn't like and I blamed him. He was changing my momma. He was taking her away from us.

Momma would eventually make a home with the new guy with us in tow and life would begin again for her. If this was what happiness looked like for her after John, have at it.

John Jr. never said a word about his father's death. I never asked how he felt about it. I never knew if he was hurt by it or relieved. We never spoke about it again.

"What Doesn't Kill Ya Makes You Strong"

I would eventually graduate high school, with honors. John Jr. would struggle a little but, he did manage to graduate on time and received a scholarship to college. I wanted to move out and work for my own way of living. I had decided that I would be independent of the drama. I wanted to make my own way in life without the help of a man and the demands of all of it. Donnie would come in and out of my life over the next few years and although it was hard to let go, I knew that I needed to. We could never have a meaningful relationship because too many things had gotten in the way by now. So, once in a while I'd play Donnie's game until I got tired and eventually I did and moved on.

I was not pleased with how things had transpired after John's drama. Momma began a new life with the new guy. She moved him in. To be honest, that's when my respect for her had changed significantly. Although he was a good provider, there was just something uneasy about him. She seemed to be happy though and for a while, that was enough for me. While I grew less dependant of her, she seemed to grow more dependent on him. Our relationship would eventually take a turn for the worst and soon I decided to just move out. I got my own apartment very quickly. I worked two jobs to secure it. By now I was almost eighteen and had no clue as to what I was doing. "If you can't live by my rules then you can't live here." Those were the last words I heard from her and I was determined to prove that I could make it on my own. It was harder than I thought. After a year, I moved back in with momma.

Donnie ran in and out of my life for about a year. I knew he wasn't good for me but I couldn't get enough. We went through every type of break up/makeup imaginable but neither one of us wanted to be the first to say good bye. We didn't and I would eventually have to move back home with momma and my Donnie drama followed. Time, circumstance and other females would eventually win out and so I soon made a conscience decision to make a life change. I moved back to Texas.

Over the years I had kept in touch with Carl and his family. One day on a long distance phone call, he asked me to come back. He wanted to explore the idea of a real relationship. He managed to convince me that I had made an impression on him years back. At the time I needed to hear that. I needed something or someone to help me get over Donnie. I needed to get out of momma's place. I just needed to get away period. I arrived in Texas on a warm June evening by previously made arrangements, to stay with Uncle Henry's daughter Kim and family. Kim had married by now and had two more kids. She worked nights and this arrangement would serve her well as she needed a babysitter. Carl and I had limited time together at first so he would drive over every weekend to see me. We took it very slow at first but his family seemed to take to me and the relationship more quickly than expected. His mom had already begun talking about the possibilities of marriage. Funny, Carl and I hardly knew each other. The last time he saw me, I was thirteen. I had it hard finding a job and the situation at Kim's house was becoming strained very quickly. I discovered that she didn't want just a babysitter as much as she wanted a housekeeper, a dishwasher and a cook.

My frustration grew stronger and stronger everyday as my money seem to run out just as fast. Right behind it was my relationship with Carl. After four months it had reached its limit. I spent two more weeks there before I decided to come back home to Chicago. Donnie's drama was anxiously waiting for me too; just like I had left it. I went right back into his awaiting arms and found myself being consumed all over again. One morning I woke up to find that I had truly had enough this time. This time was so much different than the last time. I had grown up a little and had-had my heart hurt too many damned times. Enough was enough. I broke it off for good with him and prayed to God for the strength to hold me until someone else eventually would. I trusted GOD and so I waited.

I moved back in with momma and I promised myself that it would be temporary. Her man had decided she would be a stay at home wife so he made her quit her job. They weren't really married but you couldn't tell it by her. Her attitude had changed and we stayed into it about something all the time. She was now in a position to shop all the isles of a grocery store and just like that it seemed she'd forgotten what we had been through over the years. She'd forgotten about Texas. She'd "come up" and she was not going to be quiet about it.

I kept busy praying to God to send me someone to love me unconditionally. He never said who or when but I knew Regi Cooper must be it. Well, it wasn't exactly love at first sight but it would do. I'd been celibate for almost six months and I was horny as hell. I longed for some love and affection. I was determined not to call on

Donnie ever again so after two weeks of dating Regi, I gave it up!

Reginald Adam Cooper was his name. We'd attended the same high school and had mutual friends but had never spent any time together. We ran into each other at a night club one Saturday night. We talked and got reacquainted and soon after began dating. There was an immediate connection because he had just gotten out of a bad relationship as well. It's true what they say about misery. It loves company. We had fun together when we could find time, due to my work schedule. I'd landed a third shift position and most of the time we would spend weekends together when time allowed. We grew closer very fast and soon we were in love.

Regi and I got married a few years later and had a son. My brother gave me away. Momma and I were on the outs and so she didn't attend the wedding. I was devastated. I was her oldest child and only daughter. If God could show up certainly my momma could. One of my greatest joys was becoming a mother; to have a child of my own. I wanted to be the best kind of momma and I wanted to give my child a drama free life. I made it my mission. Regi and I made a promise that there would be no arguing, no fighting in our house.

Through the years I had shared some stories of my upbringing with Regi. Some things were more embarrassing and painful to talk about but Regi made it easy to talk about them. His upbringing was so much different from mine so it made it difficult for him to completely understand sometime. He tried and that's why I loved him so.

One day, a year or so before we got married, he got a chance to see a different side of my momma. We'd returned to my house after spending the night together. I was preparing to change clothes for work. Momma had company in the backyard that day, a cook out. She had asked me to find and bring something to her as I tried to explain that I was running late for work and didn't have the time. Shortly thereafter, Regi and I heard her enter the house and mumble something in anger apparently towards me. We would soon learn, upon preparing to leave, that she had ignited a roach bomb outside my bedroom door while we were still in the house. Fumigating the house is one thing but, to commit the act in the presence of people is foul. I believe she tried to kill me.

To this day I'm not sure if jealousy played a part in it or not but, momma decided it was time that I leave her house. She never said why and I didn't ask. I packed my shit and left for good.

Our relationship had entered a place of no return but I was determined not to let it break me. Regi was willing and ready to be my solace; my refuge. He wanted happiness for me because he'd witnessed first hand what I had been up against. "Babe, you ever think about finding your real father?" Regi asked one day out of the blue. "You know, I haven't thought about it. I'm so used to not having one," I laughed. "Maybe you should think about it, seriously, this might be what you need … can't be any worse than your mother!" he laughed.

"Unforgettable"

God could not have sent me a better partner. It would take a while to understand that Regi was everything I needed. He was supportive, a solid provider and a good friend. My best friend, yet something always seemed to be missing. As much as I loved him it just never seemed to be enough. Motherhood had been more challenging than I'd thought as I had become a mother and a wife all in the same year. Being a fulltime anything is exhausting and I just couldn't find enough energy for anything outside of that. Regi desired more of my time that I couldn't seem to find between the baby, the job, the bills. Loving each other was never questionable but, Regi's appetite for the physical was more than I could bear. We often had major discussions about it. Sometimes the discussions would turn into arguments.

My sex drive was stuck in neutral and it created a lot of discomfort in the marriage. I no longer had the desire to be intimate with the man that I loved more than life it self. When we were intimate, it felt more like a task. It seemed to be just one more "to do" on my list of things for the week. Regi couldn't understand it and I didn't want him to. I didn't want him to know what I believed was the real problem. There were some things he just didn't know about me and my past and I was afraid to tell him. My stepfather didn't get the opportunity to physically take my innocents but he managed to do so mentally. I knew that my aggressions where fueled by my past and I knew I needed to understand that and remove myself from it before I lost everything.

Regi didn't know about the incident with John and I never told him of some of my episodes with Donnie either. He had no idea of how I allowed myself to be used and be made a fool of by Donnie; how often sex was used as an attempt to keep him in my life. From all of this, I began to veer sex as an empty pretence of "love" and a way to control a situation. My experiences in my life would teach me that and now it had become a major obstacle in our marriage. I hated seeing him come my way so much so that I would welcome my period. At least then, I'd be safe for at least 5-7 days.

I needed Regi in my life and in order to keep him there, I had to work through this, so I told him everything. After the shock and angry, after we'd done all of the crying we could do, we made love like there was no tomorrow. Regi took my story to heart. He was far more understanding than I had imaged. I guess he truly meant what he said when he vowed " for better or for worse". We both vowed to work this through in an effort to strengthen our marriage and our respect for one another. We were determined to be our best as a family, he as a father, me as a mother, and us as friends.

"Babe, what did you decide about finding your real father," Regi asked one day out of the blue.

"I don't know. What difference would it make now? "I replied as if to be unconcerned.

"I really think it would be good for you. It might answer a lot of questions for you; me too. I'm wondering whose side you got your nice ass from."

I was in the kitchen at the time washing dinner dishes. I turned the running water off and walked towards Regi with dripping, wet hands. "Don't get smacked in yo mouth boy," I said slapping him on the back of his head. We laughed about it and I finished the dishes.

He had me thinking that maybe this was a good idea. Momma and I were really on the outs. It had been three years now yet I was still upset about her not attending the wedding and more importantly, not being apart of our son's life. She'd missed most of the highlights and it truly made a big difference to me.

How would I do this? Where would I start? These questions seemed impossible to answer. Momma had told me long ago about my biological father. It was only when I disclosed to her that a family member had already let the cat out of the bag when I was just nine years old that she confirmed it. Although there was not much to be said, she told it, never saying anything bad about him. She would say at times that I had his skin tone. Was that all she remembered about him? Was that all I had of him? The more I thought about it the more I wanted to know.

Through coincidence and circumstance it happened. The day finally came. Shopping in the store one day, I ran into an old classmate Alicia from high school. We hadn't seen each other since graduation day and by the looks of her, time had not been kind. We hugged, laughed and talked for about an hour. We talked so long that the ice cream in my cart began to soften. Instinctively I returned it to the freezer and got another one before heading to the check out. Alicia caught up with me in the parking lot where we exchanged phone numbers and promised to keep in touch. I put the number in my purse hoping I'd never have to use it, started the car and drove away.

Two weeks later the phone rang and it was Alicia. She was surprised that I hadn't called her yet and I finally mustered up an excuse as to why I hadn't. She believed it and the conversation went as planned. "Girl, it was so good seeing you at the store. Life looks like it's been good for you. Whatcha been doing with yourself?" she said inquisitively.

"Not much," I said, not really wanting to go there with her. I was somewhat hesitant that Alicia wanted more from me. Her appearance told me there was more to her story and I really was not in the mood to get caught up. "I'm married now, three years with a three year old," I explained. We continued talking for well over an hour before Alicia would expose her truth. What I had misunderstood. Truth is she'd lost her mom just two months prior to us bumping into one another. She was an only child and she always seemed to have the best of everything when we were in school. I envied her for that. We grew close because of it. I had no sisters so it was natural for me to cling to the idea of getting close to my female friends in that way. I always wanted a sister and we were as close as sisters could be at one time. We hung out, double dated a few times but, after graduation we simply lost track. Now here we were talking like strangers at first until we could warm up to one another and I could relax a little. Over the next few months we'd talk or visit each other often. Regi seemed to enjoy having her around too. He liked the idea that I'd found an old friend. He thought it would be just as easy to find my father. So, I made up my mind to do just that with Alicia's help. One Friday evening after work Alicia called.

"Hey girl, what's up?"

"Nothing…just got in from work. What you up to on a Friday night?"

"I'm tired and I'm not going anywhere tonight."

"Got a question for you?"

"Okay …" she said with hesitation.

"I think I wanna try to find my real father. I need some help… you in?"

I'd called up one of momma's older sisters six month's earlier. Aunt Rose and momma used to hang out together back in the day. In fact, they all dated guys who were all friends. That's how momma met him. That's the story they told. Aunt Rose was more than willing to open up and let the wine of the grapevine flow. Listening to her I wondered why I never asked her about this bit of history before. "Child, you wanna know about yo daddy?" she said looking like the cat that ate the canary. "I'll tell you about your daddy if you wanna know." For some reason, she was more excited about this than she should have been. Did she feel she was about to tell momma's darkest secret or something? What ever it was, I was damned sure gonna let her.

Aunt Rose and I went on for hours. She hadn't given up anything more than momma had told me but she thought she had. Even though Aunt Rose and momma were as close as distant sisters could be, this would explain why she enjoyed this conversation as much as I did. My daddy, according to Aunt Rose was a married man and according to all accounts, momma didn't know it until she told him she was pregnant. Truth be told, all of them were married and it didn't seem to matter. Momma was different though. She had her pride. She let my daddy think that he was not the father and would decide to raise her baby on her own, that was until she met and married John.

Momma thought for some reason having me grow up thinking John was my daddy would make everything alright with the world. If she only knew. John could never be my father. I didn't look like him and I certainly didn't act like him but like momma, I believed the lie too. What you don't know won't hurt you I suppose. That's until you discover the truth.

With Aunt Rose's information and Alicia's help, we found him. Three months prior to my father's visit, we'd spoken on the phone. "So, they say we are related huh?, he said with an attempt at humor. I got it. He was trying to break the ice while I was trying to keep my cool. Keeping my cool proved to be painfully difficult because I had no idea how I was suppose to act.

"Yeah, that's what I've been told but I guess we won't know until we meet," I replied.

"Well, here's what we'll do. My wife and I usually spend our anniversary in Michigan every year. Let's make plans to meet each other then. We'll stay over and get acquainted before going over to Michigan. Sound like a plan?" he asked.

At this point it really didn't matter how it went down. I was just happy that it was happening. I agreed and then I began making preparations for their arrival. Regi was just as excited as I was. He started making minor repairs to the house so that it would look its very best. Our son technically never had a grandfather on my side of the family so it was a little exciting for him as well.

Alicia stopped by two days before they were to arrive. She wanted to meet them too but we decided to wait on that since we weren't sure just how this thing would play out. She wasn't too happy about the decision but she understood nevertheless. "Take a lot of pictures and I want to hear about everything so don't leave anything out," she yelled out the driver's window as she started her car to leave.

The day of their arrival I was nervous as a whore in church; palms sweating. I walked the house fluffing pillows, wiping off tables for the third time. Regi thought it was funny and cracked jokes when he could think of one. He finally concluded that I truly was nervous and suggested that I take a ride to calm my nerves. I did one better, I went to Alicia's. "Regi, call me when they get here. I don't wanna be here when they arrive," I said nervously. He reached out to hug me and I fell in his arms. "Am I doing the right thing babe? This is crazy. I am nervous as hell." He kissed my forehead before pushing me back slightly. "Just be yourself … it's gonna work out. Just be yourself." Regi was my rock and I trusted him with my life.

Mr. and Mrs. Anthony Parsons arrived approximately two hours after I'd left for Alicia's. As promised, Regi called me. Driving home seemed to be the longest drive of my life. Ninety-nine million pictures went through my mind about what this whole thing would look like. Ninety nine million questions accompanied every visual. Would I really look like this guy? Would we like each other? Of course we would, he's my father so he has to I thought.

He was all that I hoped he would be; tall, dark and handsome. It was just like momma had said, "his skin tone." It was that and so much more. I had his cheeks and his smile. This was my daddy and nobody could tell me different.

I would soon discover that he would not be the one to be concerned about though. Mrs. Parsons had her own agenda. It wouldn't take long for her to play her hand.

I stepped out of the car and walked to the front door and there he was, opening my door as if he lived there and I was coming to visit him. For what seemed like an eternity, we both stood across from one another in awe. There was no doubt from either of us that we were related. He stood what seemed to be ten feet tall. Carmel toned complexion and stylishly coordinated from head to toe. That's where I got it from I immediately thought.
That's where I got my style of dress. For that split second I was proud as hell. This is my daddy! For a split second I felt I had one up on John Jr. In a childish sort of way I thought, my daddy was better than his daddy. His need to excuse himself convinced me that he was overwhelmed too. He took a moment in the bathroom to pull his self together. When he returned we embraced. The emotion

that came over me that day was one that I will never forget.

The moment couldn't have played out better if I had written it myself. It was more than I could have imaged. When the dust settled we all sat down and talked. Regi once or twice gave me the signal that we made up earlier before they got there just in case I was loosing control. "Wipe your finger across your noise if you think I should pull up" is what I told him. I didn't want to get too consumed to the point that I might lose control, just in case things weren't going well. Bonnie showed her hand and Regi wiped his nose. "So, now that you've found your dad, what next?" she said with a slyness that was transparent. I got a bad vibe from her right off the top. She watched every action and every reaction my father and I exchanged from the moment we met.

"I'm not sure what you mean Bonnie," I said as if I had no clue at all what she meant. I peeped this heffa the moment she arrived. She had already made it clear, from the number of conversations my father and I had prior to their arrival, that she was running things. He would always make sure that I spoke to her before he'd end the call without fail. Hell, I was trying to get to know him first. She could just fall in where she fit in was how I saw it.

"Well, I mean, what are you gonna call him? What kind of plans do you have going forward? That kind of stuff," she said almost demandingly.

"For now I'll call him by his name, Anthony. At least until we can get use to this thing"

"Sooooo … then what are you gonna call me? She pushed.

 I pushed back, **Bonnie!**"

She looked at me with surprise. Did she think I was gonna call her "Momma?" Not!

I barely know either of you I thought. Now you got demands and expectations? There was Regi wiping his nose again. I took a deep breath and decided to clear up this mess. I said, "This is new to all of us. Let's just take things slow. I'm sure everything will work out fine."

My father and his wife left the following morning headed to Michigan to see other relatives is what they told us. We spoke again after they'd arrived home a few days later and his entire demeanor had changed. His tone was different and it was clear that he was trying to back off a little. I was in amazement but not totally surprised. Bonnie was clearly in charge and I began to see just how much. I believed she was the reason for the change in my father. The next few conversations over the next few months got really ugly to the point I found myself arguing with him constantly about his perception of my behavior during their visit. It was to be understood that I was not his first priority and that I was not his only child therefore my need to consume his time was unacceptable. What?!

It made no sense to me. What did I do wrong? What did I do to make him act this way? I was his daughter. She was just his wife. She could be replaced. Regi tried his best to console me. He refused to let me believe that I had done anything wrong and I needed to hear that from him. I was convinced that I had made a huge mistake but he kept reminding me that although it didn't fair well, it was still the right thing to do. At least I got some questions answered.

My father had allowed himself to believe that there was more to my inquiry than just wanting to meet him. In an earlier conversation he boldly asked if my mother had sent me to look for him. It took all of the strength in me not to disrespect him with a few choice cuss words. I'm a strong believer though that if you want a quick ticket to hell, cuss your parent. I knew better. My momma taught us better.

"Let's Do It Again"

It was a month before the Thanksgiving holiday and my father and I hadn't spoken in awhile. I decided we needed to just pull the plug on it. This thing was not gonna work between us. Regi was getting stressed by all of the arguments with my father and my mood swings were putting a strain on our relationship. Renard was five by now and he required more of my attention too. I needed to get back to the basics and give more attention to my husband and my son.

Thursday nights were Regi's skate nights. He loved skating. In fact, the skating rink was where we had our first date. I didn't do well on wheels so I stayed at home with Renard on skate night. Thursdays became momma and son movie night for us with pizza and the Ninja Turtle movie.

Regi was on his way out the door when the phone rang. "Babe, you want me to get that?" he yelled from the living room. "Could you please? I'm in the bathroom," I yelled back.

"Hello?"

"Ummm … hello Regi, this is Anthony."

"Ohhhh … hey Anthony, how you doing?"

I could hear Regi talking but couldn't make out who he was talking to. I dried my hands and opened the door. Regi stood in front of me with the phone extended in his hand. "It's your father," he whispered. I violently shook my head from left to right and mouthed in a whisper, "tell him I'm not here." Regi gave me that snoopy dog head tilted look then pushed the phone in my direction. I returned his look with a look of my own as he lightly kissed my forehead and waved good bye.

The conversation started out slow; both of us being ever so caution not to set it off. Past conversations almost always end up being explosive. My father had called to say that we should wipe the slate clean and try again. He wanted to be the first to extend the olive branch. He called to ask if we'd join them at their home for the Thanksgiving Day holiday. Had his conscience gotten the best of him? Had he suddenly grown a pair of balls? I didn't dare ask but I wondered never the less. In the spirit of forgiveness, I told him I'd speak to Regi and we'd get back to him in a few days.

We'd never been to Kentucky before and thought this would be a nice thing to do. We would make a family vacation of it. We decided to drive down so that Renard could feel the full effect of traveling on the road. He loved it! We underestimated the bathroom breaks we'd have to make with a five year old but it was fun nevertheless.
It reminded me of those days John Jr. and I would be as equally excited about our "road trips." It's funny how your life every now and again runs parallel.

We arrived safely and had no problem finding the house. It was a beautiful two story Georgian with a huge backyard. The neighborhood was well kept. It reminded me of the homes of the white folks momma used to clean in Texas. My father was a well kept man for all practical purposes. That was my take the first time I saw him. He looked like money though that was not so much the attraction for me. I was just proud that somebody like "that" could be my daddy. My image of a father drew from my image of John; a drunk, hustling bastard with a sensation for molesting girls. I hated John for everything he ever stood for and it did my heart good to know that momma had done well with my daddy even if he was someone else's husband at the time.

The inside of the house was just as pretty as the outside. Bonnie was very generous with the decorating. Everything matched up quite well. She appeared to be well taken care of too with her gold chains and diamond rings. A little over kill I thought but, once again, she was making a statement. We got all the bags from the car and unloaded them in the bedroom assigned to us. Bonnie had prepared a meal for us too so, I helped set the table and entertained her with small talk while the men got reacquainted. Renard was excited about the puppy they owned and insisted that we should get one.

The bed slept well. I guess the long ride tired me out because I slept like a rock. "Good morning baby. You okay?" Regi asked wiping the sleep from his eyes. "So far, so good." I replied. "If this thing goes south, we are out of here. I am not gonna see you upset again, okay?" He was serious.

We spent the morning sightseeing. My father and Bonnie wanted to show us the city and the mall. The rest of the day would be filled with some of Bonnie's family coming over for Thanksgiving dinner so we couldn't stay out too long. We had no idea others would be there but hoped that all would go well anyway. The guest started arriving about five o'clock. There were a couple of my father's relatives and a couple of their mutual friends.

Everything was nice, even the meal. We played a couple of board games after dinner and those who could keep their eyes open after the meal watched a movie. By eleven, everyone had gone home, dishes were washed and it was time to retire for the night. We were expected to leave early the next morning heading home so I was good and ready to hit the sack.

"Navie, can we talk to you and Regi for a minute?" my father asked entering the kitchen from the garage. "I'll get him and we'll meet you in the living room," I explained. Regi had gone up to the room already to wait for me. Renard had conked out an hour earlier.

"The bullshit is about to start." I said, shaking Regi to consciousness. He had fallen asleep watching t.v. "What's up?" he replied.

"They want to talk. They want us to meet in the living room," I said.

"About what? Do they know what time it is? We are leaving in the morning," he asked.

"Let's just get this over with. I know it's some bullshit. I feel it Regi…" I whispered to avoid being heard.

We met them in the living room just as we'd promised and just as I said, there was some BULLSHIT brewing. He started out subtle. She never said a word. Then he asked the question of all questions. The one question that had started all this mess in the first place, "**Did your mother have anything to do with you looking for me?**" At that moment I needed God's graceful forgiveness. I would need to say a zillion Hail Mary's. I would need to kiss the foot of the Pope and give away my first born to repent for the ass kicking they both were about to get. Regi grabbed me before I could move. He hugged me hard enough to collapse a lung. With my face turning red with angry and my teeth clinched enough to burst a vein, I took a deep breath and aimed at the both of them. "I told you before; my momma didn't have anything to do with me looking for you. I have never wanted anything more from you than to meet you with the hope that we could start a relationship. I've never asked you for anything and never expected anything. This is it!

"I am done with you and this …" Regi pulled me out of the room without saying another word. We went back to our room and packed our things. We got in our car and drove home.

That experience would change me forever. We couldn't talk about it while Renard was awake in the car. We didn't want him to know how upset I was. It was two hours into the ride home before we could talk. I cried until my heart ached and all Regi could do was hold my hand and repeat that he loved me. That magic would work in all other circumstances but it couldn't penetrate this pain. This pain was different because it came from some place deep; deeper than the incident itself. It encompassed every experience I had in my life, all of the flies in my life, the flies that lay helplessly on the window sill in my room so long ago. Wingless flies don't stand a chance in the world. One minute you're up and vibrant and the next you're on your back, down for the count. My wings had been plucked and I was down for the count. For a sad moment in time, my life rolled backward and I saw the devastation. I saw Donnie and I saw Carl. I saw Dorothy and I missed her. I saw Kent with Courtney. I saw Uncle Henry. I saw Junior with my foot in his chest and I got angrier. I saw John and everything he took from me and then I saw momma and I cried some more.

"By HIS Grace"

An older cousin once told me that GOD can bring you through anything. I believed in HIM and though we were brought up to believe in HIS existence, I never knew HIS power until I took a chance and called on HIM myself.

My father called after we'd arrived home. I refused to take the call. He finally got the message and things went dormant for a few years. Life would get back to some normalcy for us and even the relationship seemed to flourish. We'd grown too big for our tiny starter home so Regi and I decided it was time to sale. We searched high and low for a place hoping to find one before a buyer would move us out of our existing one. The house sold first and we moved in with momma until the closing of our new place. As reluctant as I was, it made the most since to just storage our things and live with her for the next couple of months. She welcomed us with open arms as if our past meant nothing at all. She was good for that. She'd cause a ruckus, I'd stop speaking then she'd call up out of the blue as if nothing had happened. I hated that. When I'm mad –I'm mad. People seem to think that they can say or do anything to you and expect you to just roll over. I've been accused of holding grudges simply because I don't believe in that philosophy. I believe that you treat as you'd like to be treated. When you've wronged someone you need to apologize, make amends. This is how hearts are mended and relationships salvaged. To regard it in a way that belittles the situation is irresponsible.

We watched what we said in momma's house and were very conscience of what we did. We stayed away as much as we could because we didn't what any trouble. That December we closed the deal and moved into our new home the week of her birthday. Renard had a big room and a big backyard to play in. All the things that I'd put on my wish list for my new home came true. We had all the room we needed and I was happy.

One year to the date of our move in, the phone rang. I didn't recognize the number on the caller ID. "Ummm, may I speak to Naïve?", the deep voice said on the other end. "This is she," I uneasily replied. The voice sounded familiar but it couldn't be I thought. "Hey …" he paused, "this is you father … Anthony." I pulled the phone from ear and looked at it as if it were a foreign object then stood there in awe. I spoke with certainty holding all emotion, "okay … what can I do for you?" First off, I wondered how the hell he got my number then secondly, what did he want now.

"I know we haven't talked in a while but, I've had this whole situation on my mind for a long time …" He went on with what seemed like forever. It began to sound like the phone conversations on the Charlie Brown series, "… *whoah, whoah, whoah*".

"So… I was wondering if you would take a DNA test."

Screech!!! What did this fool just say to me?

I suddenly woke from my trance. "Hold up. What did you just say to me?" I said in amazement. If Anthony was good for one thing, he was good for keeping shit going.

It turns out that dear old dad had a change of heart. He wanted the relationship between the two of us to work. He believed that in order to achieves this, we needed to do things right. I saw Bonnie written all over this thing. She had long gotten into his head way back when we first met and obviously her feelings had not changed. My father believed that he should do things right, the way things should have been done in the first place before moving forward with the possibility of a relationship with me and my family. To do this, he'd want me to submit to a DNA test. I let this fool continue his babble and when he was done, I said my peace.

"Let me make something very clear to you. I will honor your request, at your expense and when the test comes back and says with certainty that you are my father, don't ever call me again." I stood firm and I felt strong. For once, since the bus incident with Junior back in Tennessee, I felt vindicated and empowered.

99.97% is what the test read. After all the work I put into finding my father, a man who by all accounts never did anything for me in all my life, it boiled down to this. Momma once told the story of how persistent he was about paternity in the beginning. The story was that he'd shown up a few times at my grandmother's bearing gifts; a tricycle even. Momma would refuse them in hopes that he would finally get the message. He did when she married John. Now here we were. For someone who'd never asked him for a thing, I was now being asked to give blood to determine my worth. Doesn't that beat all?!

If it weren't for Regi, my son and the few close friends that I had helping to keep my head on straight, I would be stone crazy. I fell into a deep funk and it seemed as if it would never bottom out. I felt lost and isolated. John Jr. got himself addicted to drugs and had himself a whole set of different problems so he was in no condition to help me. Momma was being momma. One day, sitting quietly in my room, I decided to pray. I've prayed before but this time it was a little different. I needed a friend and I talked to HIM as if he were just that.

"Hey God … it's me again. I know that you're busy with more important stuff but, if you got a little time, I need to talk to you. You already know my trials and tribulations. My relationship with my mother is unbearable sometimes. She drains me Lord and I try to do all I can for her 'cause that's what I'm suppose to do. My relationship with my father, I don't understand this. I'm a good person and I do right by others. How could someone like me come from two people like this? Lord, I feel so isolated and alone sometime. I pray that you strengthen me enough to get thru this. Teach me to harbor no ill will against either of them. Mend my heart as well as theirs and move me in a direction that I may recognize those that truly love me. Lord, thank you for my wonderful husband and my beautiful son. Teach me to be the best that I can be for them. All these things I ask, I pray, in your name-Amen."

"The Rebuild"

The sun was shining bright and the air was crisp. Traffic moved swiftly as if everyone were in a hurry to be somewhere. I was at a stop, waiting for the light to turn green. The radio was down low but loud enough to hear the music. I reached to turn it up so that I could hear a little better. The light changed and I proceeded through the intersection. I thought to myself, how wonderful life really is. My marriage was going well. We were on our way to celebrating ten years together. Renard was getting excellent grades in school; honor roll even. We had jobs and drove a nice car. What more could I ask for?

Regi and I had decided that we would mark our ten year anniversary with a trip to Jamaica. Neither one of us had ever gone. That's what made it so exciting. We decided that we'd take our income tax refund and make it happen. I picked up some brochures one day in the mall and brought them home to pick out our destination.

"Hey, let's renew our vows. It's free in Jamaica," I said with excitement.

He responded, "why not!"

"Ya sure you wanna marry me agin," I asked in a childish like manner. He hesitated with a slight pause, rolled his eyes toward the back of his head as if to ponder then simply said, "absolutely baby."

Regi always knew how to make me smile. Sometimes he'd be silly about it and then some times he'd just simply do the sweetest things. Flowers, cards, notes left on the seat of the car. What ever he thought would remind me that I was loved, he'd do it. Ten years came and went so fast. Jamaica was the perfect place to renew our vows and fall in love all over again. During the ceremony I cried as if it were the first time. That moment in time brought to me a real understanding that this was where I wanted to be, with him, until God said otherwise.

Life and the circumstances it subjects you to, show you which direction you should be going in. But when you run over or into the potholes, sometimes you get your head bumped and you come out of it delusional, confused even. All my life I'd been subjected to unwarranted circumstances. I've stepped in a few potholes and I knew the road that I was destined to ride was truly not the path set for me. I always felt indifferent. Not simply by my look, my walk or my talk. There always seemed to be more to it and people knew it. I knew it. Some people confused it with arrogance among other things. They thought that I was somewhat stand offish. I was simply guarding myself from the potential pain that people so unselfishly bestow on others. I began to understand that it was by God's grace that I survived all that I had. I could have followed the path that momma chose. I could have married a man exactly the same as John. After all, we do as we see to do; creatures of habit. HE had a plan for me though and I knew that if I kept fighting for victory, it would be mine to claim.

Before I could move on with my quest to free myself, I needed to settle things with momma once and for all. Time had done its job and we'd become more civil and tolerant of each other. Time and maturity brought me to a place where I believed that in order to mend the fence with her, I had to come clean with my true feelings and my truths.

I called momma one evening after settling in from a long day at work. She was occupied by her favorite evening t.v. game show. "Hey", I said nervously as she picked up the phone on the second ring. "Hey yourself," she replied. Before long we were off and running with our normal stride of covering all of the family gossip she'd captured over the week. She loved gossip and it didn't matter who it was about. If it was juicy, she was telling it and often added a little flavor to it for the best affect. Twenty minutes or so of this finally netted me an opportunity to bring up what I'd actually called for. I wanted to tell her about the DNA test I was asked to take some time back. I'd chosen not to mention it to her at the time because to do this, I would've had to tell all; particularly about John. It wasn't the right time then but, now was the time because I had more courage to do so.

I was always afraid to speak up or speak out for fear that John would hurt her-bad. Over the years as the fights intensified between the two, each episode seemed to come with accelerated violent behavior. Once during one of their altercations, John attempted to kidnap me as a way of revenge. Momma had refused to go back to him this particular time after one of her many attempts to leave him. John thought that if he took me she'd change her mind. Thank God my uncle was there to save me, that time. She gave in and soon after went back to him once again. I don't think she ever thought about the mental scars I would be left with. She never asked me or John Jr. how we felt about any of it but, I was prepared to let her know about all of it. Right here, right now.

"Momma, I need to talk to you about something important" …

In retrospect, I should have kept it to myself. Maybe not say anything to her about it at all but, I did. I got the reaction I thought I would but in reality I'd hoped for something different. "I wish you would have told me when it happened, I would have killed that bastard" is what she said. That angered me more than the act itself because I believed she knew. She knew but, it's so much easier to turn a blind eye when the consequences are greater if you speak up, speak out about it and the shame is simply too much to bare. As for my "sperm donor" and the DNA test, not much value to that response either. I left the conversation feeling torn and confused but relieved that I had accomplished shifting the blame back to the owner. I felt the freedom of releasing all that stuff that didn't belong to me, back to momma. She'd done this to me. None of this was my fault and I could freely say it would certainty, I DID NOTHING WRONG! God had stepped in and helped me speak the words. This to me was the beginning of living again and in that single moment I felt sorry for my momma. She really didn't get any of this at all. I cried myself to sleep that night with Regi holding me. I wasn't crying for me though. The tears I shed this night were for her because I knew we could never be on the same level of thinking as long as I lived. Something went terribly wrong during those days of John. I wasn't the only one who got damaged by him in the end. John had destroyed my family as I knew it, forever.

"Rewarded By Truths"

Two o'clock one Sunday afternoon my seventeen year old baby boy walked across the stage to receive his high school diploma. The proudest day of my life, except for the day he was born. Renard was always considered my blessing unexpected. Regi and I had tried several times to conceive early in our relationship but each time proved unsuccessfully. No hormone pill would do it. It took one hot July afternoon on the living room floor for it to happen. Nine very unpleasant months later, Renard was born. I prayed for a boy. I just couldn't risk having a baby girl being subjected to anything remotely similar to my own experiences. I thought a boy would be safe and stand a better chance in the world.

And there he was. Looking just like his daddy, confident and proud. I cried through the entire ceremony. It was hard to believe that we were responsible for this day, this special moment in his life. My dream was always to be the best mom I could possibly be for my child and Renard complimented my efforts by his own accomplishments on this beautiful day. He had the tenacity and desire to be great and he was well on his way. College was the next stop.

Renard was prepped for the idea of college before he could even spell it. In my mind, it was the only way he'd have a fair chance in this world. I didn't want his life to begin or end in the spiral of messes mine had gone through. Neither Regi nor I had more than a high school education. We did okay financially but there were times when things were a little tough and struggling was common place. Together we made a conscious decision to clear up anything that might financially compromise Renard's chances of attending college. It was stressful at best but we realized that the payoff would far surpass the sacrifice.

"Renard, I am so proud of you. I know that I promised that I wouldn't cry …" I whimpered.

"C'mon mother. People are waaaaatching," he replied with a sarcastic comedic like response. We laughed. I turned to retrieve my camera to take a family photo when Renard grabbed my arm in an attempt to get my attention. He leaned over unexpectedly and hugged me. He whispered, "mom, in all seriousness, thank you for all that you have done for me. I'm gonna make you proud. I love you." He kissed my cheek and before I could speak, the tears rolled from my eyes. "Son …" I replied. "I am always proud of you no matter what you do in life. Today is your day to be proud of yourself for all that you have accomplished. Thank you for telling me that. I love you too."

I had to be the happiest parent in the room. Momma was at the graduation and I couldn't help but wonder if she'd ever felt what I felt today. I wondered if for a split second she understood the bond that I shared with my own child and if she felt she had somehow missed her own opportunity with her own children. John Jr. was having a rough time with his life. One failed marriage and his ongoing battle with substance dependability. He had children of his own but proved to be every bit lacking in the traditional sense of being a participating parent in their lives. As my only sibling, I expected John Jr. to play a more significant role in Renard's life as well but, that proved to be too much to ask for.

He was so consumed in his own quest for identity that he missed the opportunity to be better than his father was to him. For this, I finally realized that John Jr. was truly affected by John too. All the things that I saw and experienced with John being in our lives reflected on how my brother responded to his own children and to my son.

In the past, John Jr. and I hardly spoke of John. Never did he show any emotion to me one way or the other about his feelings. Perhaps he and momma talked and I just wasn't aware. Perhaps he just never said anything to anyone at all, but his actions said it all.

I never questioned his pain simply because I was so consumed with my own. In my pain I looked for my own comfort not realizing that to some degree I owed it to my little brother to look out for him as well. I guess I failed him in that way but, I can't take responsibility for anything past that. We both had the same opportunities growing up. Sometimes I felt he'd gotten things easier than I since John was "his" father. Nevertheless, we chose different paths in life and sometimes that's just the way it goes.

My wish was that John Jr. would take advantage of the opportunity to be closer to Renard, his only nephew but, that didn't happen. My son would be cordial to his uncle in his presence although he was noticeably uncomfortable around him most of the time. Thank goodness his father would prove to be one of a few men in his life to help guide him in his own way. It would be my brother's loss though once again and as he continues to struggle to find his way, I continue to pray for his recovery.

My own life turned out well. Confidence in myself and people, continue to strengthen and grow. No longer do I doubt myself or second guess who I am. Regi and Renard remind me everyday of what real love is and what being loved truly means. We've become a praying family because we know prayer changes everything.